Marcus has never been down a wormhole but, just like Felicity Frobisher, he has had a very naughty friend. He is an expert on space and the stars and has also written books for grown-ups.

'This is one of the best books I have ever read. This could go far!!!!' Nine-year-old reader

FELICITY FROBISHER

and the Three-Headed Aldebaran Dust Devil

MARCUS CHOWN

Illustrated by Ned Jolliffe

faber and faber

First published in 2008
by Faber and Faber Limited
3 Queen Square, London WC1N 3AU

Design by Mandy Norman
Printed in England by CPI Bookmarque, Croydon

A CIP record for this book
is available from the British Library

ISBN 978–0–571–23903–0

2 4 6 8 10 9 7 5 3 1

To Billie and Bobbie,

Thinking of you always and hoping
that, wherever you are, Jock and India
Paddington are keeping you safe.
(Hope you like this better than my
'I once had a very bad cold' story.)

Love,
Marcus

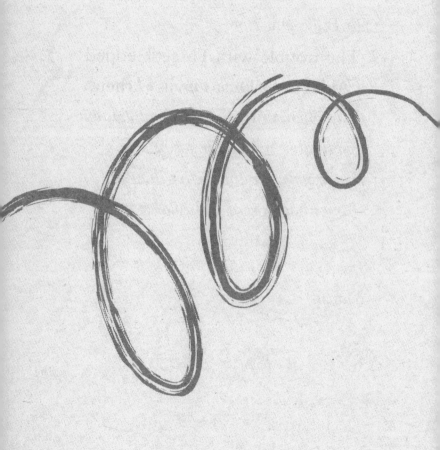

The trouble with Three-Headed
Aldebaran Dust Devils is they
dust things up and if you happen
to have one as a friend it's always
you that gets the blame on
account of them being
totally invisible.

Three heads are better than one

There was a time when Felicity Frobisher could not have told a Three-Headed Aldebaran Dust Devil from a newly wedded Capellan toast weevil. But that all changed the morning she awoke to see a patch of her flowery bedroom wallpaper wavering like a mirage on a hot summer's day.

Her first thought was that she had strained her eyes by watching too much

TV the night before. But, when she put on her glasses, the wavery patch did not go away. On the contrary, it remained exactly where it was, hovering about halfway between the floor and the ceiling, about the size and shape of a dustbin lid.

Curious rather than concerned, Felicity pushed back her covers and stepped out of bed. However, the tips of her toes had hardly touched the carpet when the wavery patch stopped wavering. *Thank goodness for that*, she thought, relieved.

But her relief was short-lived.

Though the wavery patch had stopped wavering, it had not, as Felicity fully expected, changed back into an ordinary, well-behaved piece of bedroom wallpaper. Far from it. It had transformed itself into the mouth of a long black tunnel. A long black tunnel, what's more, with stars twinkling at the far end!

Now, nobody expects a long black tunnel to open up in their bedroom wall – especially one filled with stars. But this, as it turned out, was just the first of many surprising things that the day had in store for Felicity Frobisher. As she stared, eyes wide, mouth so agape that a squadron of bees could have flown in, looped the loop and flown back out again, there was the most appalling commotion.

It sounded like a badger falling down a chimney. Only badgers don't fall down chimneys. And, if they do, they certainly don't shout 'OoOoOoO!' and 'Whoaoaaaa!' and 'Look owwwttt!'

In a panic, Felicity threw herself under her bed. Seconds later, peering out from behind a corner of overhanging duvet, she saw something shoot out of the mouth of the tunnel like a champagne cork from a bottle. She couldn't actually tell what it was because it was shrouded in a thick cloud of dust. But whatever it was, it hit the floor with a thud so hard it made the windows rattle.

'Felicity!' came her mother's voice from downstairs. 'What in heaven's name are you doing up there?'

Felicity was too shocked to answer. And, even if she hadn't been too shocked, thick dust had got into her eyes and up her nose. Instead of screaming, which is what she desperately wanted to do, she sneezed violently.

'Bless you!' said a squeaky voice.

Oh, my goodness! thought Felicity. *Someone is in my room!* Not only had they burst from a tunnel in her bedroom wall but they were *actually* talking to her! Felicity sneezed again, this time so fiercely it almost blew her glasses off.

'Bless you!' said the squeaky voice again.

Oh, my goodness, thought Felicity. *Where is it coming from?* By now, most of the dust in the air had settled on the carpet. But, even though the air was clear again, from her vantage point under her bed Felicity could still see nobody at all in her bedroom.

'"Bless you" *is* the expression used on Earth, isn't it?' said the squeaky voice. 'I mean to say, this *is* Earth?'

'Er, yes,' croaked Felicity from under the bed, stunned that she had actually responded to such a ridiculous question – and from someone she couldn't even see either.

'Well, thank goodness for that,' said the squeaky voice. 'For a moment I thought I'd taken a wrong turning at the Horsehead Nebula. It's so much harder than you think, you know, making wormholes go where you want them to.'

'Wormholes?' said Felicity, still frantically trying to locate the source of the voice. Was it in her wardrobe? Or

hiding behind her chest of drawers? Or
hidden in her collection of fluffy
animals?

'Short cuts through space-time, of
course,' the squeaky voice replied, as if it
was something absolutely everybody
knew. 'Look, you can come out from
under there. I really am quite harmless.'

'But where are you? I mean, *who* are
you?'

'Flummff,' said the voice.

'*Flummff?*'

'Yes, Flummff. *Who* are you?'

'Felicity,' said Felicity.

'Fel-ic-it-y,' said Flummff. 'What a
peculiar name.'

'No more peculiar than Flummff!'
said Felicity. 'I've never heard of such a
name.'

'You obviously haven't travelled. It's

the third most popular name where I come from.'

'And where is that?'

'Aldebaran-4.'

'I've never heard of it.'

'You really haven't travelled, have you?' said the voice. 'It's a small, extremely dusty planet orbiting the red giant star Aldebaran. I think you'll find it's in your constellation Taurus, the Bull.'

It was all too much for Felicity. She couldn't have been more confused if she'd been asked one of those maths questions about it taking two men three hours to dig a hole four metres deep. 'But *where* are you? I can't see you at all.'

'Of course you can't. I'm a Three-Headed Aldebaran Dust Devil. And, as everybody knows, Three-Headed

Aldebaran Dust Devils are completely invisible – apart from all the dust they kick up, of course. Look, Felicity, I really am totally harmless. *Please* come out from under there.'

Slowly and cautiously, Felicity emerged from her hiding place. When she saw the terrible state of her bedroom she groaned. Dust coated absolutely everything – the furniture, the windows, her favourite stuffed toys. The carpet looked as if it hadn't been hoovered in the past thousand years. What in the world would her mother say?

As if on cue, a muffled voice came from downstairs. 'Felicity! What *are* you doing up there? You'll be late for school. If you don't come down at once, I'm coming up to get you.'

'Look, I really must go,' said Felicity, snatching up her dust-covered school clothes and heading for the bathroom.

'Ouch!' squeaked Flummff. 'Watch where you're walking!'

'Sorry!' said Felicity, stopping dead in her tracks.

'We're always being trodden on,' said Flummff, resentfully. 'It's the biggest drawback of being an invisible Three-Headed Aldebaran Dust Devil.'

'Yes, I expect it must be,' said Felicity, not very sympathetically. Something suddenly occurred to her. 'You haven't *really* got three heads, have you?' She would have asked the question before but, what with all the other peculiar things she was seeing and hearing, she had let it pass.

'Of course we have,' said Flummff. 'Why do you think we're called Three-Headed Aldebaran Dust Devils?'

'Well, I thought it was just a name . . . I didn't think you *really* had . . .' She trailed off, overwhelmed at having to take on board so many impossible things before breakfast. Finally, she said, 'But why *three* heads?'

'Isn't it obvious?' said Flummff.

'Not to me.'

'Three heads are better than one.'

'Of course. How silly of me,' said Felicity, unable to keep the sarcasm out of her voice.

'Felicity!' came her mother's voice on

the stairs. 'Have you got someone up there?'

'Look, I have to go,' hissed Felicity. But, before she could get across the room, her bedroom door burst open. The dust, which had only just settled onto the carpet, was whipped once more into a mini-tornado.

'*Felicity!*' screamed Felicity's mother. 'What the devil have you done to your room?'

2
'Come back, you hooligan!'

Life is so unfair! Felicity thought as she hurried through the local park to school. Dusting and vacuuming were her two least favourite activities – right up there with doing French homework and PE. And her mother had forced her to dust and hoover every last nook and cranny of her bedroom before leaving for school.

And it wasn't even her fault. But what

was she supposed to say when her mother burst into her bedroom and saw the appalling state it was in? 'It wasn't me, Mum, it was a Three-Headed Aldebaran Dust Devil!' Try saying that next time your mum tells you off for making a mess – and see how far *you* get.

By the time Felicity had finished the dusting and hoovering, there was no time for breakfast, not even a snatched

biscuit and a sip of tea. Nor was there time to grab any sweets from the sweet jar in the kitchen, which was bad news for Felicity's health and well-being. Only by handing over a daily tribute of sweets did Felicity avoid being beaten up by the school bully, Jennifer Tetley.

Felicity was hungry and tired and almost certainly going to be late for school. *Surely my morning can't get any worse?* she thought, as she passed the swings. But, even as she thought the thought — and isn't this always the case? — her morning did indeed get worse.

On the path up ahead, an elderly park keeper with a black and gold peaked cap was raking leaves and empty crisp packets into a neat cone-shaped pile. As Felicity approached, she became aware that something peculiar was happening to the air above the pile. It was wavering like a mirage on a hot summer's day. 'Oh no, not again!' she groaned.

She watched helplessly as a tunnel opened up in mid-air. Only this time there was no constellation of stars twinkling at the other end. Instead, Felicity could have sworn she caught a glimpse of something far more familiar – *her own spotlessly clean bedroom*!

There was no time to ponder how ridiculous it was to see the interior of her bedroom while in the local park because something came tumbling out of the mouth of the tunnel in a swirling tornado of dust. The park keeper watched in dismay as his neat pile of leaves and crisp packets spiralled high into the air. He took off his cap and scratched his balding head. For a while he was totally baffled by what had happened. Then he noticed Felicity, standing in front of him, clutching her school bag and looking *very* uncomfortable. A vague understanding seemed to dawn. '*You!*' he said, narrowing his eyes. 'You did this, didn't you?'

Felicity was too stunned to answer immediately. For the second time today she was being blamed for something she  hadn't done. 'Oh no, it wasn't me,' she said. 'It was –' But, as soon as she began, she realised there was not the slightest point in saying what it *really* was. The trouble with Three-Headed Aldebaran Dust Devils, she was discovering, was that when they dust things up it's always you that gets the blame, on account of them being totally invisible.

'You're not going to get away with this, young lady,' said the park keeper as leaves and crisp packets rained down on their heads like over-sized confetti. He made a sudden and determined lunge at her. She dodged around him, surprising herself by her speed — she was the least athletic girl at her school — and dashed out of the park gate. 'Come back, you hooligan!' the park keeper shouted after her. 'I'll get the police on you!'

3
The ladies in the lake

Only when she was several hundred metres down the road did Felicity finally risk stopping. Leaning against a garden fence and wheezing, she looked back the way she had come. The elderly park keeper was standing by the park gate, waving his fist furiously. *Thank goodness he was too old to chase her.*

She took off her misted-up glasses and wiped them on her sleeve. She was

a well-behaved child, dull and boring.
Trouble and Felicity Frobisher simply
never went together. Never had she been
chased out of a park by a fist-waving
park keeper!

Felicity had just about recovered her
breath when she sneezed violently. The
thought crossed her mind that there was
suddenly rather a lot of dust in the air.
But, before she could put two and two
together, she heard a squeaky voice.

'*Flummff!*' she exclaimed, in a strop.
'Did you *have* to mess up those leaves?'

'I couldn't resist it,' said Flummff. 'It
was such a neat pile. It *needed* messing
up.'

'You mean you did it *on purpose*?'
Felicity was incredulous. She had

assumed Flummff didn't have complete control of where his wormholes went – that his emergence above the pile of leaves was an accident, some kind of navigational mistake. It had never occurred to her he had ruined that poor park keeper's day *deliberately*.

'It was just a bit of fun, Felicity,' said Flummff.

'*Fun!* You could have got me arrested. I might have been taken away in a police car. I might have been locked away in a cell. I might have . . .' She trailed off, not absolutely sure what the police did to you after they put you in a cell.

'Police car?' said Flummff. 'Cell?'

Felicity was far too irritated to explain. 'Look, w*hy* are you following me?'

'I'm bored.'

'Bored!'

A lady, walking past with two baby beagles, shot Felicity a very odd look.

'*Bored?*' she hissed into the empty air.

'You've no idea how boring it is on Aldebaran-4,' said Flummff. 'Nobody there ever wants to play. It's the dullest, dreariest planet in the whole universe. I travelled halfway across the Galaxy because I thought it would more fun on Earth.'

Felicity shook her head in disbelief. If anyone had asked her why extraterrestrials might want to visit Earth, she probably would have said to learn about human civilisation or maybe even use their superior technology to stop wars and make Earth a better place. Never in a million years would it have occurred to her that they might come halfway across the universe *because they were bored* – because on their home planet *there was no one to play with*.

'Look, I'm going to be late for school,' said Felicity, brushing off the latest layer of dust which had accumulated on her school uniform. She headed for a nearby bus stop, which was across the road from an ornamental lake. She knew Flummff was following her because she could feel the draught on the back of her legs and because she could hear the rustle of leaves swirling about on the pavement behind her. She was still a little cross but her curiosity got the better of her. Over her left shoulder she said, 'What *exactly* is a wormhole?'

'A short cut through space. Didn't I tell you?' said Flummff. 'You go in one mouth, travel just a little distance and when you come out of the other mouth you find you've gone a long, long way.'

Felicity digested this. 'And you can make a wormhole go anywhere?' she said.

'Just about. Look, I'll show you.' Flummff vanished – as much as it was possible for someone who was already invisible to vanish!

'*Where are you?*' hissed Felicity.

A bus was drawing up as she arrived at the bus stop. With a swish the automatic doors sprang back and the person at the head of the queue – an old lady with two heavy shopping bags –

stepped forward. Only something very odd was happening to the air near the door. When the old lady stepped up, she never actually ended up on the bus. Instead, her leg vanished in mid-air, then the rest of her. Felicity watched, first in amazement, then horror, as first one, then two, then every person who had been in the bus queue, stepped into . . . well, into absolutely nothing at all!

'*Flummff, where have they gone?*' But there was no need for an answer. Screams and frantic splashing sounds were coming from the other side of the road. One by one, the bus passengers, led by the old lady with the two heavy shopping bags, were appearing out of thin air – in the middle of the lake!

A lorry driver leapt from his cab. He waded past startled ducks and geese and began helping the poor, sodden ladies out of the water. Even the elderly park keeper was hobbling down the road towards the scene. 'Oh my goodness,' said Felicity when she spotted him. With her head down and one hand hiding her face, she hurried away. '*Flummff!*' she hissed. 'Did you *have* to do that?'

'You asked whether I could make a wormhole go *anywhere.*'

'I know. But I didn't expect you to

show me. Not like *that*.'

'It *was* fun, you've got to admit.'

'*Fun!*'

There he was, talking about *fun* again. The trouble with Flummff, Felicity was beginning to realise, wasn't only that he dusted everything up and then escaped any blame by being invisible most of the time. The trouble with Flummff was that he was actually very, very *bad*.

Felicity was now in the safety of a side street and the terrible commotion in the lake was far behind her. Nobody,

thank goodness, had chased after her. And nobody had arrested her. 'So, have I got this right?' she said. 'You came to Earth down a wormhole just like the one you sent those poor ladies through?'

'Exactly,' said Flummff. 'The Galaxy is actually crisscrossed with them. It's like a pan-galactic Underground system.'

'And you can travel absolutely anywhere you like through a wormhole?'

'Anywhere – well, almost anywhere.'

'What do you mean, *almost anywhere*?' said Felicity. 'Where *can't* you travel?'

'Er, won't you be late for school, Felicity?'

'Oh my goodness, yes!'

'Where is your school?'

'There,' she said, pointing up the hill to where the clock tower of Inchley Manor School poked above the red rooftops of a sprawling housing estate.

'Follow me,' said Flummff.

The air in front of Felicity started bucking and twisting like soft toffee being pulled first one way then another. Moments later, the mouth of a tunnel opened up. At the other end, she could see the hedge-lined driveway that led up to her school.

'Flummff? *Flummff?*' she shouted. But he had already gone.

'Come on,' came an echoey voice from inside the wormhole.

'I *can't*,' said Felicity. 'I *really* can't.'

'You'll be late.'

Felicity had a momentary vision of the dreaded Miss Steerpike with her glass eye standing at the school gates, glaring at the latecomers with her good eye while inscribing their names in the dreaded Late Book. That was all it took. 'Wait, Flummff. Wait, I'm coming.'

4
'Hand over your sweets!'

Daylight vanished, to be replaced by an eerie white glow, like the inside of a giant electric light bulb. 'Ooo, I don't like this,' muttered Felicity. 'I *really* don't.' She had an overwhelming desire to get back out onto the street. But, before she could do anything about it, the ground beneath her feet gave way.

She was falling, falling head over heels down a steep tunnel.

'Whoahhhhhh!' she cried as she collided with a wall. To her surprise, she actually bounced off it. It felt soft and squidgy – almost like a living thing. She hit another wall and bounced again. The ridiculous thought flashed through her mind that this was exactly what it must have been like to be swallowed by a dinosaur, gulped down the cavernous gullet of a hungry Tyrannosaurus rex!

The walls of the wormhole were semi-transparent and, as she ricocheted back and forth, Felicity caught tantalising glimpses of the world beyond the wormhole. Great shadowy shapes were swimming about out there like monstrous sharks.

The shark-shapes aside, plummeting down a wormhole was no more frightening than bouncing on a bouncy

castle. In fact, Felicity was
actually beginning to enjoy
herself. That may have been
a mistake because, without
warning, the wormhole
started to get a whole lot
steeper. 'Oh no-o-o-o-o!'
she wailed. She caught a
brief glimpse of
daylight below. And
was promptly
coughed out into the
school privet hedge.

Even as she
fought to
disentangle herself
from the
branches, she
could hear the
blood-curdling

voice of Miss Steerpike, demanding to know the name of some unfortunate wretch who had committed the unforgivable crime of sleeping through their alarm or missing the bus to school. Miss Steerpike was down at the bottom gate. At any moment, she might look up from the Late Book and catch Felicity in the no man's land of the school driveway. Quickly, Felicity brushed the leaves off her clothes – together with yet another coating of dust. She took a deep breath and scuttled away towards the safety of the school buildings.

The bell must have gone, because the playground was deserted. Avoiding the school's main entrance – where Mr Floggitt, the headmaster, had his office – Felicity headed for the side entrance, which was usually more lightly guarded.

She skirted the wall of the science block
and hurried across the netball court. She
passed the woodwork room, turned the
corner by the bike shed – and ran smack
bang wallop into Jennifer Tetley and her
gang.

Jennifer Tetley was 'hard'. Even the
boys were scared of her. There was a
rumour she ate broken glass for
breakfast and had put her stepdad in

hospital by hitting him over the head with a china model of the Blackpool Tower. Jennifer Tetley was flanked by her two most feared lieutenants, Virginia Creeper and Kerry Gold. She blew a huge pink bubble-gum bubble and sucked it back into her mouth. 'Sweets!' she demanded, her hand outstretched.

'I-I-I didn't have time to get any,' stammered Felicity.

Jennifer Tetley's eyes blazed menacingly. She spat her bubble gum out and it landed on Felicity's left shoe. Felicity didn't dare remove it. 'Sweets!' Jennifer Tetley demanded again.

'Or you'll be sorry,' added Virginia Creeper.

'*Very* sorry,' reinforced Kerry Gold.

Jennifer Tetley took a threatening step closer to Felicity. But something was happening to the air between them. It had begun to waver in a most disconcerting manner. Uncertainty and confusion flashed across Jennifer Tetley's face. But there was nothing she could do to stop herself. Her forward momentum carried her into the mouth of the wormhole. There was a scream, which got smaller and smaller as if Jennifer Tetley was disappearing down a deep well, and then the wormhole snapped shut behind her.

'Jennifer!' screeched Kerry Gold.

'Oh my God!' screamed Virginia Creeper.

All Felicity could mutter was: 'I'm sorry, I'm late. I've got to go.'

Only when she had reached the school's side entrance did she dare to look back. What met her eyes was a most peculiar sight. Kerry Gold and Virginia Creeper were scrabbling about on their hands and knees, tapping the ground and desperately trying to locate the secret trapdoor down which they were utterly convinced Jennifer Tetley had fallen.

5
'I'm telling you, a wombat bit me!'

The morning's lessons got started only
after the fire brigade had brought
Jennifer Tetley down from the school
roof. She made a pitiful sight up there,
sobbing as she clung desperately to the
flagpole on top of the clock tower. When
the extendable ladder crept up towards
her and a yellow-helmeted fireman went
up, slung her over his shoulder and
brought her down, the whole school

cheered (everything was captured by a
roving TV crew, which had rushed to the
scene). Partly the cheers were for the fire
brigade, for spicing up a dull schoolday
with such an exciting and dramatic
rescue. Partly they were because
somehow – and nobody quite knew *how*
– the school bully had been brought
down to size.

Jennifer Tetley's mother was summoned
by the headmaster and arrived clad in a
pink leather trouser suit, teetering on six-

inch-high purple stilettos. Mr Floggitt gave her instructions to keep Jennifer Tetley at home for at least a week to recuperate from her ordeal. How she got onto the school roof was a mystery. Jennifer Tetley was too distressed to speak about it. It was left to Miss Steerpike, who had done an Open University degree on German interrogation techniques in the Second World War, to try to get to the bottom of it. She made Kerry Gold and Virginia Creeper stand on one leg and balance glasses of ice-cold water on their heads while she shone a bright torch into their eyes. It was all to no avail, however. Miss Steerpike was unable to get the slightest bit of sense from either of them.

When lessons finally did get under way, it was boring geography. Felicity's class was so abuzz with excitement that Mr Slashandburn had to yell at the top of his voice, then threaten a triple homework assignment on irrigation techniques in south-central Uzbekistan, before he could get everyone's attention.

Felicity had had more than enough excitement for one day – more than enough excitement for a lifetime, in fact. She had found herself a desk at the very back of the class and was desperately trying to make herself as small as possible in the hope that no one would notice her. She wasn't succeeding. Kerry Gold and Virginia Creeper, fresh from their interrogation by Miss Steerpike, were sitting only a few desks away, eyeing her suspiciously.

Mr Slashandburn spun a globe, stopped it abruptly with his index finger and announced that the subject of today's lesson would be Australia. Felicity, who was only half-listening, was beginning to harbour the faint hope that Flummff had got bored with Earth and returned to Aldebaran-4. The hope was dashed, however, when something  caught in her throat. The next moment it was as if a Martian dust storm had descended on the classroom. Felicity, and everyone around her, was convulsed by uncontrollable fits of coughing.

Mr Slashandburn was on the spot instantly, waving his arms about like a demented windmill in an attempt to clear away the dust. 'Who – *cough* – did this?' he spluttered. 'Who – *cough, cough* – is responsible?'

'Felicity – *cough* – Frobisher,' said Kerry Gold.

'Felicity – *cough, cough* – Frobisher,' echoed Virginia Creeper.

'Felicity Frobisher,' said Celia Snitch. She wasn't even sitting near by, but telling on people was her speciality and she wasn't about to let Kerry Gold and Virginia Creeper take her crown.

'Is it true?' asked Mr Slashandburn.

'Oh no, sir,' said Felicity. 'It wasn't me. It was –' But, of course, there was no point in finishing the sentence. That was the trouble with Three-Headed Aldebaran Dust Devils. Whatever *they* did, it was always *you* that got the blame.

'Felicity Frobisher, I'm disappointed in you – *very* disappointed,' said Mr Slashandburn. 'You've always been such a model, well-behaved pupil.'

It was true. Felicity was a good girl and had never been told off by a teacher before. Her face was hot with shame and embarrassment and it was something of a relief when Mr Slashandburn ordered: '*Out!* Get a broom and clean this mess up *right now*!'

This is getting to be a habit today, Felicity thought bitterly as she swept between the desks. Flummff had clearly not got bored with Earth. He had not gone back to Aldebaran-4. *He's actually in this classroom now*, she thought. Imagining what mischief he might get up to in the next half-hour brought her out in a cold sweat.

When Felicity had finished sweeping and sat back down at her desk, Mr Slashandburn was telling the class how Australia had been isolated from the rest of the world for millions of years, and how that isolation had resulted in the evolution of a host of unique animals and plants. One such plant, he said, was the eucalyptus tree, of which there were apparently more than six hundred species.

'I can get you one of those,' said a squeaky voice.

'*Flummff!*' exclaimed Felicity, loud enough to cause Kerry Gold and Virginia Creeper to swivel round in their seats. Felicity had to take a sudden and unnatural interest in fingernails until she was sure they had turned back.

'Flummff!' she whispered. 'Where are you?'

Out of nowhere, a eucalyptus branch, heavy with thin, waxy leaves, dropped onto her desk. 'Oh my goodness!' cried Felicity, grabbing it and stuffing it as quickly as she could under her desk. To her immense relief, nobody else had noticed it.

'Don't you like it?' said Flummff.

'*No, I don't!*'

'But I went all the way to Australia to get it.'

'*Please* don't bother,' said Felicity crossly.

Mr Slashandburn had now moved on from plants to animals and was talking about kangaroos, of which there were apparently uncountable millions hopping about the Australian continent.

'Would you like a kangaroo?'

'No!'

'*Two* kangaroos then?'

'Now you're being silly. If I don't want one kangaroo, I hardly want two, do I?'

'Not even if they're small kangaroos?

'No!'

'You're no fun.'

'*No fun!*' Felicity was incensed. 'It might be fun for you but it's nothing but trouble to me. Ever since I got out of bed this morning, you've been getting me blamed for things.'

'I saved you from the school bully,' Flummff reminded her.

'Well, yes, you did, and I'm grateful for that,' said Felicity. 'But, actually, if you hadn't made such a terrible mess of my bedroom in the first place, I wouldn't have had to hoover it and been late leaving home. And, if you hadn't made me even later by annoying that park keeper and dumping all those poor ladies in the lake, I wouldn't have had to go to school through a wormhole. And, if I hadn't done that, I wouldn't have bumped into Jennifer Tetley in the first place.'

Mr Slashandburn had exhausted all he had to say about kangaroos and was describing the egg-laying duck-billed platypus. 'And I don't want a duck-billed platypus either,' Felicity said sharply.

'I wasn't going to get you one,' said Flummff.

'Good, that's just as well then, isn't it?'

'I thought Earth would be much more interesting than this.'

'Well, I'm *sorry* but that's really not my problem.'

Mr Slashandburn obviously didn't know much about duck-billed platypuses, apart from the fact that they were one of the only mammal species that laid eggs, because he had swiftly moved on to wombats. Although wombats looked furry and cuddly, he said, they actually had sharp teeth and could give you a very nasty nip.

'If you like, I could send your teacher to Australia.'

'*Please* don't.'

'It'd be fun.'

'*No, it wouldn't.*'

'Oh, I'm *so* bored,' said Flummff. 'I think I'll go back to Australia.'

'What a good idea,' said Felicity rather uncharitably. But, hardly had she uttered the words, than an alarming thought sprang into her mind. *No, he wouldn't, would he? Surely he wouldn't?*

'*Flummff!*' she hissed.

But there was no reply. He had already gone.

Felicity held her breath and prayed. For what seemed like an eternity nothing happened. Then there came a piercing scream from Sharon Fruit, who was sitting next to Celia Snitch. On her lap had materialised a round ball of grey fur. It leapt to the floor and headed like a fluffy guided missile for the trouser leg of Mr Slashandburn. He was so startled by the sight that he stood rooted to the spot rather than running for his life, which would have been by far the most sensible thing to do.

6
A deskful of Moondust

On her way to double science, Felicity passed the door of the headmaster's office, which was open wide. 'Don't be ridiculous, man,' she heard Mr Floggitt saying. 'You must be mistaken.'

'I'm telling you, headmaster, there was a wombat in my classroom – look what it *did*.'

Felicity caught a brief glimpse of Mr Slashandburn's rolled-up trouser leg and below it on his shin an angry red splotch which looked as if someone had squirted tomato ketchup. Wincing at the sight, she hurried on past. She hoped she wouldn't be blamed for *that* as well.

The bad news was that Flummff was almost certainly following her to her next class – there was a faint trace of dust in the air. Fortunately, the really bad dust storms that accompanied Flummff's emergence from a wormhole seemed to be short-lived. She could only guess that it was that last, extra-steep stretch of tunnel that caused all the problems, shaking up Flummff like a filthy duster.

'Did you *have* to go and get that wombat?' Felicity hissed out of the side of her mouth. 'You *knew* I didn't want one.'

'But, Felicity,' Flummff protested, 'you said you didn't want a kangaroo or a duck-billed platypus. You never said anything about not wanting a *wombat*.'

'*Flummff!*' she spluttered. 'You really are *impossible*.'

Mr Crucible, the science teacher, told Felicity's class that it was National Astronomy Week so he would be showing a film about the Apollo Moon landings. Felicity was actually quite relieved by this. In the dark, anything bad Flummff decided to do would most likely go unnoticed.

The lights had gone out and on the screen a fuzzy, space-suited figure called Neil Armstrong was standing by the lunar module, which had evidently just deposited him on the Moon. 'This is one small step for man,' he was saying, over a crackly radio link to Earth, 'one giant leap for mankind.' Seeing the crater-strewn lunar surface prompted Felicity to ask a question. 'What's it actually like on Aldebaran-4?' she said.

The last thing she had expected Flummff to say was that he would actually take her to Aldebaran-4 to see – but of course he did. 'Oh no, I couldn't,' protested Felicity.

'Why not?' said Flummff.

'I'm *in a class*,' she said. 'What if Mr Crucible noticed?'

'He won't – it's too dark,' said Flummff.

'Oh, I don't know,' said Felicity, who was wishing she had kept her stupid mouth shut.

'Go on, be a devil,' said Flummff. And added: '*Like me!*'

'I'm really not sure –'

'That's settled then,' said Flummff annoyingly.

'No, really, I don't think –'

But it was too late. The mouth of a wormhole had opened up by the side of her desk. Felicity could see it shimmering by the light of the film being projected up on the screen.

'Come on,' said an echoey voice.

He really is a bad influence, she thought and, against her better judgment, shuffled along her seat. With a deep breath, and with her heart in her mouth, she dived head first into the waiting wormhole.

Though she knew what to expect, it didn't make the experience of taking a short cut through the space-time continuum any the less weird. As she ricocheted back and forth down the soft squidginess of the wormhole, she saw the same monstrous shadows as before circling in the gloom beyond the translucent walls. But now they had been joined by tiny luminous stars which were flitting back and forth like fireflies between the shadow-shapes. Had they been there before? Surely she would have noticed them if they had? While she was still pondering this matter, the wormhole suddenly steepened and she was spat back out into normal space.

To her immense surprise she found herself *floating* in mid-air! She was in a giant hollow cylinder, the walls of which were made of sheets of metal bolted together. Large portions of them were covered with chunky switches and coloured lights, some of which were winking on and off. 'Is *this* Aldebaran-4?' said Felicity uncertainly.

'Don't be silly!' chided an echoey voice. Flummff must still be inside the wormhole. 'It's your International Space Station. I thought you might like to see it, so we've stopped off on the way.'

'I don't believe it – I'm in the *International Space Station*!' said Felicity as she drifted past a beady-eyed video camera mounted on the wall. Her stomach felt very peculiar indeed, as if she was sky-diving down a bottomless well, and she had absolutely no control over where she was going.

There was one small, square window in the cylinder. Through it, something extraordinarily bright was shining. It

took her a while to come abreast of the
window but when she did, Felicity let
out a gasp. Outside, more beautiful than
any sight she had ever seen, was a
dazzlingly brilliant world of blue and
white. It was her own planet – Earth!

If only she could have lingered for an hour or two and just gazed at that ravishingly gorgeous sight. But Felicity had no idea how to stop herself and, before she had time to identify a single continent beneath those porridge-white clouds, she had floated on by.

Up ahead there was a sudden commotion. The end of the cylinder had a circular hatch, which Felicity hadn't noticed before, and an astronaut in a red T-shirt was squeezing himself out of it like toothpaste from a toothpaste tube. He was closely followed by a second astronaut. 'I don't believe it, Buzz!' exclaimed the first astronaut when he saw Felicity floating there. 'It's a little girl!'

'Holy mackerel, Randy,' said the second astronaut. 'How the hell did she get up here?'

Felicity found it odd being talked about as if she wasn't there. Within a few seconds, however, she *really wasn't there*. It all happened in a blur. An echoey voice shouted 'Quick!', the air in front of her went all wavery and suddenly she was back in the wormhole and falling again.

Behind her, in the International Space Station, a voice crackled over a loudspeaker: 'This is mission control. Did we hear you say you've got a *little girl* up there?'

Buzz and Randy, who had been staring with disbelief at the place where Felicity had been but was no longer, exchanged dumbfounded glances. Then, they shook their heads in unison.

'There's no girl up here,' said Buzz.

'You must have misheard us, mission control,' said Randy.

Felicity had no time whatsoever to think about her time on the International Space Station, nor about how incredible it was to be actually up in space looking down on the Earth revolving below rather than sitting in double science. The reason was that she was abruptly spat out of the wormhole, this time into a raging storm.

A hail of grit blew against Felicity's glasses and she had to put her hand over her mouth just to breathe without choking. In the sky, half-obscured by dust, a giant red sun hung like a huge blood orange. It was by far the dustiest place Felicity had been in her life.

Surely, *this* was Aldebaran-4? If there was the slightest doubt in her mind, Flummff promptly confirmed it.

'Welcome to my planet,' he said proudly. 'What do you think of it?'

'It's – er – lovely,' said Felicity, not wanting to appear rude.

Actually, it was awful. While she stood rooted to the spot, dozens of mini-whirlwinds zipped back and forth all around her. She didn't know where to look. It was like being stranded in the

middle of a motorway intersection. She felt terribly dizzy, and that was on top of being sand-blasted and half-suffocated.

'All these whirlwinds –' asked Felicity, pawing away the dust which was getting in her ears and up her nose. 'They're all Three-Headed Aldebaran Dust Devils like you?'

'Every last one of them,' said Flummff. 'At the last count there were eight billion of us on Aldebaran-4.'

'*Eight billion!*' The thought made Felicity feel even dizzier.

'Come on, Felicity, I'll show you around.'

Felicity, who had not dared to move from the spot in case a Three-Headed Aldebaran Dust Devil accidentally ran her down, had seen enough already and desperately wanted to return to Earth.

She was wondering how to say this to Flummff without sounding impolite when a giant whirlwind, tall as a tornado, detached itself from all the other whirlwinds and headed directly towards them. 'FLUMMFF?' boomed a voice like the voice of God. 'IS THAT YOU?'

'*Quick!*' squeaked Flummff. And before she could say anything Flummff had bundled her back into the wormhole and she was falling, falling back to Earth. Only when she was safely back at her desk in the darkened classroom did she finally get to ask, 'Flummff, who *was* that?'

'Oh, nobody,' said Flummff.

'What do you mean, *nobody*?' said Felicity.

Up on the screen at the front of the

classroom, a spacesuited Harrison Schmitt from Apollo 17 was using a geologist's hammer to break an orange rock in two. 'The Genesis Rock,' said the film's narrator, 'was the key to unlocking the secret of the Moon's origin.'

'I can get you one of those,' said Flummff hurriedly.

It was obviously an attempt to distract her by changing the subject. But, before she could utter a word, he had gone. The next moment there was a terrible commotion as a whole bucketload of rocks rattled down onto her desk. '*What in the world's going on back there?*' yelled Mr Crucible, stopping the film and clicking on the classroom lights.

Felicity felt like a cornered animal that had nowhere to escape. With no possible way of explaining where the rocks had come from, there was nothing she could do but look as innocent as she could and plead total ignorance. She would never have guessed she would get away with it, but she did.

What saved her was Mr Crucible's total and unexpected fascination with the rocks. From the moment he picked up the first one and examined it with his magnifying glass, he was utterly engrossed. So engrossed, in fact, that when the bell went for the end of the class,

Felicity was able to get up from her desk and actually creep past him to the classroom door. He was still miles away in a world of his own, shaking his head and muttering over and over again, 'This is astonishing, absolutely astonishing!'

7

'The BEST French accent I've ever heard'

During the lunch break, much to Felicity's great relief, Flummff got up to no more mischief. Afterwards, he followed her to French, where Miss Cross announced she would be going around the class and asking everyone to say what they wanted to do when they grew up. She began with Celia Snitch, because she was sitting at the front of the class. '*Bonjour, Celia,*' said Miss Cross.

'*Bonjour, Mademoiselle Cross,*' said Celia Snitch.

'*Qu'est-ce que tu voudrais faire quand tu seras grande?*' ['What do you want to do when you grow up?']

'*Quand je serai grande, je voudrais être une espionne internationale*' ['When I grow up I want to be an international spy'], said Celia Snitch, not surprisingly.

Felicity dreaded French. Miss Cross, who in thirty-seven years of teaching French had never been known to smile, had said that Felicity had the worst

French accent she had ever heard, a remark which had not exactly done much for Felicity's confidence. To distract herself from her inevitable humiliation when her turn came around, Felicity hissed, '*Flummff?* There's something about you that puzzles me.'

'What?'

'How did you learn *English*?'

'Oh, that's easy,' he said. 'I've got a pan-galactic speaking dictionary.'

'A *what*?'

'You don't have them on Earth?'

'Of course we don't.'

'I wouldn't be without one,' enthused Flummff. 'Every pan-galactic speaking dictionary is programmed with all the languages spoken on all the known planets in the Milky Way. I'm actually talking to you in Aldebaran, you know, but it automatically comes out in English.'

'Wow!' said Felicity.

'Do you want to have a go?'

Un homme de feu...

In the next row, Brian Nylon was saying that when he grew up he wanted to be *un homme de feu* [a man of fire]. Miss Cross corrected him: '*Un pompier* [a fireman], Brian.' Next up was Terry Lean, followed by Trevor Dick (who was good at everything). After that, it would be Felicity. 'Does your pan-galactic speaking dictionary know French?' Felicity hissed urgently.

dig!

ahem...

'Of course it does,' said Flummff.

'Then yes,' said Felicity, surprising herself, '*I want to have a go.*'

Miss Cross turned to Felicity and smiled. It was the weary smile she always reserved for Felicity. It signalled that she was prepared for imminent and inevitable disappointment, that her expectations were rock bottom. '*Bonjour, Felicity,*' said Miss Cross. '*Qu'est-ce que tu voudrais faire quand tu seras grande?*' ['What do you want to do when you grow up?']

Felicity's heart was racing. Her mouth was so dry it felt — well, like felt. She wasn't at all confident that this would work. She looked about her at the expectant class and the weary Miss Cross. Taking a deep breath, she said, 'When I grow up I want to be an astronaut on board the International

Space Station. I will be floating in zero gravity and watching the Earth, blue and white against the inky black of space.' Only it came out in French, beautiful, fluent French: '*Quand je serai grande, je voudrais être astronaute à bord de la station spatiale internationale. Je flotterai dans la gravité zéro et je regarderai la Terre qui apparaîtra bleue et blanche contre la profondeur noire de l'espace –*'

Miss Cross's jaw dropped in amazement. Her eyes welled up with tears – tears of joy. For the first time in thirty-seven long years of teaching, a smile broke out across her hardened features. 'Oh my darling,' she declared, rushing to the back of the class and throwing her arms around Felicity. 'My little darling. Your French is so beautiful. Where did you learn it? Have you been

practising secretly in your spare time?'

Felicity was taken aback. One minute she was being severely told off by a teacher, the next she was being hugged like a long-lost child. 'I think I just somehow got the hang of it,' she said lamely. Only, of course, she said it lamely in French, not English. And every word she continued to speak, until the bell finally went at the end of the class and Flummff switched off the pan-galactic speaking dictionary, was in the most beautifully accented French Miss Cross or anyone else had ever heard.

8
A short cut through the space-time

The door to the headmaster's office was ajar as Felicity passed by on her way to PE. 'Thirty-seven years I've been in the teaching profession,' she heard Miss Cross saying. '*Thirty-seven years*, and I have never – *never* – known an improvement in a pupil as miraculous as in Felicity Frobisher. I tell you, Mr Floggitt, if I die today, I'll die a happy woman. Oh, the perfection of that girl's

French accent, the pure heavenly perfection . . .'

Maybe having a Three-Headed Aldebaran Dust Devil as a friend was not so bad after all! Felicity thought.

Miss Sprint sent them on a cross–country run while she stayed in the warmth and comfort of the changing room with her feet up, picking between her toes with a toothpick and flicking through the latest issue of *Practical Tank Maintenance* (she was in the Territorial Army and at weekends drove heavily armoured vehicles across Salisbury Plain).

The outward leg took them across the 'Scruff Lots', a wasteland of scrubby woods, marshy ponds and skiploads of abandoned household rubbish. One moment they were battling their way through chest-high brambles, the next they were having to thrust aside rusting prams and dented washing machines as they half-waded, half-swam through thick black mud the consistency of treacle.

By the final leg of the route, which took them back to school along the South Inchley Bypass, polluted by exhaust fumes, Felicity was red in the face and gasping. Filthy lorries thundered by as she lumbered along, dripping mud and trailing an old toaster by an electrical lead which had somehow snagged on her ankle.

Everyone had passed her long ago.

Everyone, that is, except Kerry Gold and Virginia Creeper. A moment ago, when she had looked back the way she had come, Felicity had noticed them sitting on the kerb making rude gestures at passing motorists.

Felicity, who was very probably the most unfit person in the whole school, was close to total physical collapse. She had developed a painful stitch in her side which meant she could run only in

short, stuttering bursts. Most of the rest of the time she had to walk and occasionally – like now – she staggered to a complete halt. She was bending double to get her breath back – and trying to detach the irritating toaster – when someone shouted her name. Startled, she looked up, just in time to be slapped in the face by a wall of air as a bus flew by only inches away. At the back of the bus, waving through the window and laughing their heads off at her, were Kerry Gold and Virginia Creeper!

Cheats! Felicity thought. She knew

their game because they played it so often. Just in front of the school there was a big oak tree. Kerry Gold and Virginia Creeper would get off the bus and wait behind it. When most of the runners had gone by, they would splash themselves with water to make it look as if they had been sweating, then stagger, exhausted, past Miss Sprint on the finishing line.

Felicity was a good girl and had never cheated at anything in her life. But the sight of Kerry Gold and Virginia Creeper flying past her like that — and *laughing* at her — well, that was simply *too* much. 'Flummff!' she called. '*Flummff!*'

When she didn't want him, he was always around. *Where was he when she needed him?*

She ran a bit, walked a bit and

stopped again. But Flummff still failed to make an appearance. She had just about given up all hope when she was hit by a blizzard of dust. At first, she thought the dust had been kicked up by a revolving cement-mixer lorry which happened to be passing by at the time, but blizzards of dust from passing lorries do not speak. 'Felicity?'

'Where have you *been*?' said Felicity.

'Isn't it obvious?' said Flummff.

'Not to me.'

'You've been wading up to your neck in water. And Three-Headed Aldebaran Dust Devils absolutely *hate* water.'

Of course they do, thought Felicity, feeling stupid that it hadn't occurred to her. Dust devils were made of dust, weren't they? If they ever got water on them – well, who ever heard of a *mud devil*? 'Flummff,' she said, 'can you get me back to school?'

'Of course I can!' said Flummff. He was so eager to help that the air in front of Felicity began to waver almost immediately. 'I was going home to Aldebaran-4 but now I think I'll stay,' he said.

Oh no, thought Felicity, *I've encouraged him*. But she jumped into the wormhole anyway.

The driver of a large articulated lorry almost choked on his custard-filled chocolate doughnut. '*Did you see that?*' he said to the man in the passenger seat, pointing at the pavement with his doughnut.

'See *what*?' said the man, looking up from his newspaper.

'I swear, one minute she was there and the next –'

The man in the passenger seat looked at him oddly.

'I think I'd better get my eyes tested,' said the lorry driver.

In another place – another universe even – Felicity was falling, falling. It seemed that hardly any time passed at all before she tumbled out onto hard, gritty asphalt.

Even before she had picked herself up and dusted herself down, Felicity realised her mistake. She had forgotten to tell Flummff *exactly* where she wanted to go. Instead of depositing her at a safe distance from the school, so she could wait, like Kerry Gold and Virginia

Creeper, for everyone to finish the cross-country run, then hobble past the finishing line, he had dropped her smack bang in the middle of the school driveway. It was too late to dash back out of the school gates.

'*Felicity?*' said Miss Sprint incredulously. She had finished *Practical Tank Management* and come out to greet the early finishers. 'I don't believe it. You're the first one back. Normally, you're last.'

Felicity was speechless.

'You've cheated by taking the bus, haven't you?' said Miss Sprint.

'No!'

'Don't lie to me!' said Miss Sprint. 'That makes the cheating even worse.'

As if things weren't already bad enough for Felicity, at that moment

Sharon Fruit, the fastest girl in the class, sprinted up the school driveway.

'*Felicity?*' she said when she saw Felicity standing there. 'I thought I passed you *ages ago*.'

'That does it,' said Miss Sprint, her face hardening beneath her bleached Number One haircut. 'Detention for you, Felicity Frobisher! You're staying after school today to write lines.'

9

Flummff has a visitor

Felicity had never been kept behind after school before. And she couldn't even complain that it was unfair. She was no better than Kerry Gold and Virginia Creeper. In fact, she was *worse*. Not only had she cheated on the school cross-country run but she had cheated and been *caught*.

The job of supervising Felicity's detention was entrusted to Miss

Steerpike. Fortunately, Miss Steerpike was also supervising an inter-school netball tournament in the playground. So, after fixing Felicity with her glass eye and leaving her in no doubt of the terrible torture that awaited her if she ever cheated again, Miss Steerpike left Felicity to her own devices in an empty classroom.

Felicity had just written 'I must not cheat in cross-country runs by taking the bus' for the 178th time when the inevitable happened. For once, however, she was not unduly worried. Miss Steerpike had said she would be back in an hour and, by then, all the dust Flummff kicked up would surely have settled out of the air.

'It's *so* boring in here' was Flummff's first observation.

'It's *meant* to be boring,' said Felicity, suppressing a cough. 'I'm being punished.'

There was a pause while Flummff evidently took this in. 'But you don't *really* want to be stuck in a classroom, do you?'

'Of course I don't.'

'Well, let's go, then!'

'You know I can't. You'll get me into even more trouble.'

'*Go on,* Felicity,' insisted Flummff. 'Don't be a scaredy-cat.'

'A *scaredy-cat*! Where did you get *that* phrase from?' But, of course, even before he told her, she realised: his pan-galactic speaking dictionary. 'Anyway, I'm not scared,' protested Felicity.

'Yes, you are.'

'No, I'm *not*.'

But, by protesting that she wasn't scared of going with him, she realised she'd actually talked herself into *going*. He'd made her do it on purpose, she was quite sure. He was *so* annoying. 'Look, promise you'll get me back here before Miss Steerpike notices?'

'Yes, of course I promise.'

How good was a Three-Headed Aldebaran Dust Devil's promise? Well, there was only one way to find out. Felicity collected up the pages on which she had painstakingly written those 178 mind-numbing lines. She couldn't quite believe she was taking such a huge risk in leaving the classroom during detention. What had come over her today? 'Where are you taking me?' she asked, her voice trembling with apprehension.

But he had already gone.

Felicity's fourth trip down a wormhole was every bit as disconcerting as the previous three. But this time, when she tumbled out at the other end, she was pleasantly surprised that her fall was broken by soft sand. She must be on a beach because she could hear the sound of the sea behind her. She twisted around to take a look – and a wave promptly crashed over her!

PLOP!

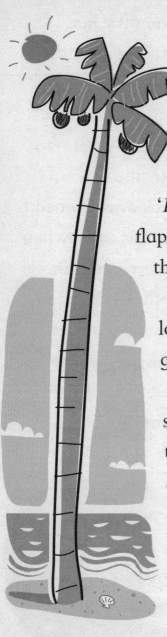

'*Oh, no!*' Not only was she soaked but so too were the sheets of paper on which she had written her lines!

'*Flummff!*' she said crossly, flapping the pages vainly in the warm air.

'You should have looked where you were going.'

'I don't believe it!' she said, aghast. 'Don't you take the blame for *anything*?'

'You'll dry out. Don't make a fuss.'

'*Don't make a fuss!* Really,* Three-Headed

Aldebaran Dust Devils were the *most exasperating* creatures. Felicity pawed the wet hair from her eyes and blew ineffectually on her soggy, ink-smudged sheets. She looked around. 'So where are we?' she said.

The beach was empty. It was fringed by spindly palm trees and sloped down to a sea which was more turquoise than any turquoise Felicity had ever seen.

'Hawaii,' said Flummff.

'Wow!' said Felicity. For a moment she forgot her soggy clothes. This had to beat being in detention in a dull classroom back at school.

She wasn't, as she had first thought, totally alone on the beach. A solitary surfer was in the sea. He was lying flat on his board and paddling out through the waves. Felicity walked towards the back of the beach and sat down on the warm sand, flattening her papers onto her knee. In the only patch that was even remotely dry, she squeezed her 179th line. When she looked up, she saw that the surfer had now caught an incoming wave and was standing up on his board. Felicity was idly watching him weave hypnotically back and forth through the surf, when, without warning, he vanished!

She leapt to her feet as if she had been stung. *Oh my goodness*, she thought, her hand flying to her shocked mouth. *He's been eaten by a shark!*

Moments later, however, a surfboard exploded out of thin air barely a dozen paces from Felicity. It jammed itself into the sand, catapulting the surfer clean up the beach. The poor boy, who was lucky

not to break any bones, looked back in
horror at his surfboard, which was
sticking out of the beach at an alarming
angle like a piece of modern sculpture.
He didn't even notice Felicity watching
him. Instead, terrified, he turned and fled
up the beach. '*Flummff*, can't you behave
yourself for once?' said Felicity crossly.

'It was just a bit of fun,' said Flummff.

'*A bit of fun!* You frightened the life
out of him.'

'He'll get over it.'

Felicity shook her head in frustration. There was no getting through to Flummff. It didn't matter how much she protested. Nothing appeared to curb his bad behaviour. 'Well, *please* don't do it again,' she said lamely, sitting back down on the sand to finish her lines.

Hawaii! she thought, staring out to sea and shaking her head with disbelief. Who would have thought, when she got out of bed this morning, that before the day was over she'd be sitting on a tropical island in the middle of the Pacific Ocean? Or, for that matter, that she would have experienced weightlessness on board the International Space Station? Or travelled halfway across the Galaxy to a not-very-pleasant planet orbiting the red giant star Aldebaran?

The thought of all the amazing places she had been today prompted a question. 'Flummff?' said Felicity.

'Yes,' said Flummff.

'You know before, when I asked you if you could go anywhere with a wormhole, and you said you could go *almost* anywhere?'

'Ummm,' said Flummff suspiciously.

'And remember that you changed the subject when I asked where can't you go?'

'Er, yes.'

'Well, tell me — *where* can't you go?'

'*EARTH!*' boomed a voice like the voice of God.

Felicity jumped to her feet, scared out of her wits. A great tornado of dust had materialised in front of her. In fact, it looked like three intertwined tornadoes. It towered above her like a genie out of a bottle, kicking up sand and spattering her glasses with grit. She tried to back away but, as she did so, it spoke to her. 'DON'T WORRY, FELICITY,' the tornado boomed. 'THERE'S NO NEED TO BE AFRAID.'

It knew her name!

'Wh-wh-who are you?' stammered Felicity.

'FLUMMFF'S DAD,' said the booming voice.

'Oh,' said Felicity.

'I EXPECT YOU'RE

WONDERING WHY I'M HERE.'

'Um, yes,' said Felicity.

'TELL FELICITY WHY I'M HERE, FLUMMFF,' said the booming voice.

When Flummff spoke it was in a voice that was even smaller and squeakier than normal. 'To fetch me home to Aldebaran-4, Dad,' he said.

'AND *WHY* IS THAT, FLUMMFF?'

Flummff's voice was now so small Felicity couldn't hear what it was he had said.

'SPEAK UP, FLUMMFF,' thundered Flummff's dad.

'Because I'm not supposed to come to Earth, Dad.'

So *that* was why Flummff changed the subject when she asked where he *couldn't* go with a wormhole? It all made sense to Felicity now. *He wasn't allowed to go to Earth!*

Earth was classed as a 'nursery world', explained Flummff's dad. This didn't make a lot of sense to Felicity until he went on. Apparently, there were thousands of space-faring races in the Galaxy. Each had arisen on a world much like the Earth and each had arisen in isolation from the rest. Being in isolation turned out to be important. It meant that when a race finally conquered space and sailed out from its home world to join all the other space-faring races, it had something special and unique to contribute to galactic community life.

Everything would be wrecked, said Flummff's dad, if 'contact' were made with the Galactic Club too early. For instance, if people on Earth learnt that wormholes were possible, it might make them give up the struggle to build bigger and faster space rockets. They'd get lazy and there would be no more technological progress. It was for this reason that Earth had been designated a nursery world, a planet off-limits to all space-faring races so that its inhabitants could develop in peace without any interference from outside.

According to Flummff's dad, a network of wormholes connected the inhabited worlds of the Galaxy. It was the pan-galactic Underground system

Flummff had mentioned earlier. But that Underground system completely avoided Earth. 'THERE IS A TOTAL BAN ON ANYONE COMING HERE,' said Flummff's dad. 'AND FLUMMFF, BY VIOLATING THAT BAN, HAS BROUGHT SHAME ON ALL THREE-HEADED ALDEBARAN DUST DEVILS.'

Goodness, thought Felicity. She'd assumed Flummff had only upset the odd park keeper, teacher and surfer. Imagine annoying *eight billion* Three-Headed Aldebaran Dust Devils as well!

'I'm sorry, dad,' said Flummff, in his tiniest, squeakiest voice again. But his dad ignored him.

'HE'S A VERY BAD DUST DEVIL,' said Flummff's dad. 'AND I'M VERY SORRY HE'S RUINED YOUR DAY,

FELICITY.'

'Oh no,' said Felicity, not wishing to be disloyal to Flummff. 'It's not been a bad day actually. It's been quite – er – *interesting*.'

And Felicity's interesting day was not over yet. Not by a long chalk. Flummff's dad said that Flummff's mother had been worried sick about him and was desperate for him to return to Aldebaran-4 as soon as possible. But, before that could happen, said Flummff's dad, there was one thing that Flummff must do. 'TAKE FELICITY HOME!'

Felicity didn't remember anything about her final passage through a wormhole – the trips were beginning to be routine by now – but she certainly remembered her emergence back into her classroom. Miss Steerpike was

actually waiting for her, arms folded
across her chest, face like thunder.
'Where have you been?!' she roared.

The netball tournament must have
finished early or Flummff must have got
her back too late. It hardly mattered
which, since there was nothing
whatsoever Felicity could do about it
now.

Miss Steerpike was so cross she didn't seem to register that Felicity had just emerged out of *absolutely nowhere*. But she did notice Felicity's dress and blouse, which were plastered to her skin because they had still not completely dried. And she did notice the horribly crinkled sheets of paper on which Felicity had written her smudged lines. 'What the devil have you done with your lines?' demanded Miss Steerpike, heading towards Felicity.

But she didn't get very far.

The air between Felicity and Miss Steerpike was wavering in a most peculiar manner. Miss Steerpike saw that something was wrong but it was too late. Like Jennifer Tetley before her, her forward momentum carried her into the mouth of the wormhole. There was a strangled scream which got smaller and smaller. Then Felicity was left alone in the classroom. She let out a huge sigh of relief. 'Thanks for saving my life, Flummff,' she said.

'Any time,' said Flummff. And then he said, 'Well, I'd better be going.'

'I suppose you'd better,' said Felicity.

'It's been nice knowing you,' said Flummff.

'And you,' said Felicity. She thought she was just being polite. But, to her surprise, it suddenly occurred to her that she might actually *miss* him. Having a Three-Headed Aldebaran Dust Devil for a friend wasn't all bad, she reasoned, and he'd certainly given her a day she would never forget. 'Bye, Flummff,' she said. But there was no answer. He had already gone. Probably, he was back with his dad and they were already halfway to Aldebaran-4. To the empty classroom she said, 'Don't make a wrong turning at the Horsehead Nebula!' And laughed uncontrollably.

The light was still on in the headmaster's office as Felicity crept out of school. She could hear an exasperated Mr Floggitt on the phone. 'But, Miss Steerpike,' he spluttered, 'I saw you supervising the inter-school netball tournament barely half an hour ago. How in the world did you get to be in a phone box in *Hawaii*?'

10
Unexplained incidents

Felicity had never been more glad to get home from school. The only problem was explaining to her mother why she was so late. 'I don't believe it!' her mother exclaimed when Felicity told her. 'First, you half-destroy your bedroom, then you get caught *cheating* in a school cross-country run. Whatever else have you been up to today?'

Felicity thought it best not to mention

all the other things.

Her father was in the living room, reading a newspaper with the TV on. He had a habit of not noticing anything that was going on around him, so it was a big relief to Felicity to plop down in the armchair next to him. 'Do anything interesting at school today?' her father asked, looking up from his newspaper.

'Just the usual,' said Felicity.

'That's nice,' said her dad, going back to his newspaper.

Tea was pasta, rice and mashed potatoes on a bed of puff pastry – with a bread roll (Felicity's mother was going through a carbohydrate phase). Felicity ate it in silence on a tray on her lap.

On the TV a newsreader was talking about a spate of unexplained incidents which had occurred in South Inchley today. Felicity nearly choked on her bread roll when the TV programme suddenly cut to the elderly park keeper with the black and gold peaked cap. He was standing by the lake and describing what had happened to the unfortunate bus passengers. The camera turned to a woman who was still dripping wet. She said, 'I stepped onto the bus and the next

minute I was swimming for my life ...'

Next, they showed the fire brigade getting Jennifer Tetley down from the school clock tower with their extendable ladder. And, as if that wasn't bad enough, the programme then switched to an RSPCA inspector with a heavily bandaged thumb. He had suffered the injury, he said, in the course of cornering and capturing a *wombat,* which had been terrorising shoppers along South Inchley High Street. There followed an interview with the owner of a local wildlife park, who said he was absolutely sure they hadn't lost a wombat, and also with a zookeeper at the local zoo, who said exactly the same. 'The origin of the wombat remains a total mystery,' said the newsreader, ending the item.

If Felicity thought this was the end of her ordeal by TV, she was much mistaken. Now the newsreader had turned to a guest sitting beside him in the studio. It was *Mr Crucible*!

Mr Crucible had brought in a fist-sized orange rock which he showed to the camera. 'I've had it checked out by experts at South Inchley Science Museum,' he said. 'And there is no doubt about it – it definitely came from the Moon.'

That was enough! Felicity couldn't take any more. She jumped to her feet and took her half-eaten tea into the kitchen. She deposited it in the rubbish bin and poured herself a glass of water to calm her nerves. When she got back to the living room, the local news was, thankfully, over. Now it was the main national and international news. She sat back down. She was *safe*.

The introductory music died down and the newsreader, a woman this time, looked up from her sheaf of notes. 'The top story tonight,' she announced. 'NASA, the American space agency, claims it has evidence the International Space Station is being haunted by a little girl . . .'

'Ah!' exclaimed Felicity, jumping up so quickly she knocked her water over and caused her father to look up from his newspaper.

'Sorry,' she said and escaped upstairs.

In her bedroom, she put on her nightie and got into bed. *What a day!* she thought. *Thank goodness it's over.* Relieved beyond measure to be in the safety of her own bedroom, she opened a book she was halfway through. She had read about a page and a half when she became aware of something happening at the edge of her vision. A patch of her flowery wallpaper had begun wavering like a mirage on a hot summer day just like it had done this morning. 'Oh no! Not again!' she groaned as, predictably, the wavery patch turned into a tunnel with stars twinkling at the other end.

Fully expecting Flummff to tumble out in a whirlwind of dust, Felicity

pulled the covers up to her eyes. But
Flummff didn't tumble out and there
was no dust. Instead, out fluttered a
scrap of dust-streaked paper. It winged
its way over to her bed like a sycamore
seed and came to rest on her covers.
Gingerly, she picked it up. There was a
message on the paper. In grubby,
smudged letters, it said: 'I'll be back!'

THE END

FELICITY
FROBISHER'S
Fun Facts

If you fell feet-first into a black hole, you'd be stretched out like a long strand of spaghetti.

The first rockets didn't have toilets so astronauts had to wee in their spacesuits. (Very smelly!)

Space is 30 kilometres from your doorstep – straight up! (If it wasn't straight up, you could walk there)

The Sun is big enough to swallow a million earths.

If you were in space without a spacesuit, you'd freeze, suffocate and explode!

If you could drive a car to the Moon, it would take about a year to get there.

The Moon was born when it was torn from the Earth billions of years ago.

On the way to the Moon, the Apollo 8 astronauts had to dodge balls of vomit flying around their cabin — one of them had been sick on the launch pad!

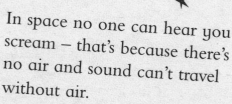

In space no one can hear you scream — that's because there's no air and sound can't travel without air.

Some scientists think life on Earth originally came from Mars inside a meteorite — so you could be a Martian!

Acknowledgements

Thanks to Grace, Richard, Rosie, Tim, Sam and Jamie.

Also Karen, Sara, Karen Gunnell, Julia Wells, Donna Payne, Mandy Norman and Lucie Ewin.